I0699781

Working Blue Press

Second Edition

ISBN 979-8-9887672-9-9 (Kindle)
ISBN 978-1-967038-00-8 (Print)

For all the women who love good sex,
and all the meals you've eaten while
talking about it with good friends.

Content

Suggestions for Further Reading

Girls Who Brunch Erotic Series Books 2, 3 and 4.

Follow Lacey Love on Amazon to keep abreast of new releases!

One Egg, Two Sausages

Girls Who Brunch Erotic Series

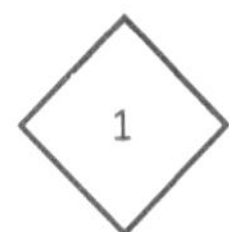

1

One Egg, Two Sausages

Annie slid into the red leather booth with a happy huff as she pulled off her aviator sunglasses, tossed her long, blonde hair and threw her brunch companions a shit-eating grin that was lit up by the devilishness in her green eyes.

"Nice diamond necklace," they each murmured with questioning eyes.

"Thanks," she said as she absent-mindedly fingered it with a smile, then launched into her good news. "I had a threesome last night."

She waited for each of their three reactions, predicting them as they came. First, as always, was Summer, who sat right next to her.

Her long, black hair was glossy and straight, and her rich, brown eyes were filled with a competitive congratulations. Of the four of them, she and Summer were the two that wanted to tell the best sex story at the weekly girl's brunch. The sucking sound she made with her teeth indicated she was not about to be bested.

"Well done," she said. She picked up her champagne flute and nodded a cheers to Annie before taking a slow sip of the citrus mixed with Moscato. She leveled a stare over the rim as her breasts heaved a little with her congratulatory sigh.

She can't beat my threesome. Not this one anyway.

Across from Annie was Tabitha, a plus-size dream boat and hair stylist who always had a new color, cut, or extensions, depending on the latest fad. It didn't matter what

framed her gorgeous face, she was
a knockout, and the lucky men who
got to roll around in the sack with
her knew it. She also loved to say
the word fuck. A lot.

"Dying," she said as a Cheshire
grin lit her ice blue eyes. She gave
today's extra long chocolate brown
extensions a seductive shake. "I
need every fucking detail."

As she leaned in to hear the tea,
the waitress popped over, so she
leaned back.

"Sweetie, give us five," Tabitha
breathed.

"Sure," the young redhead said
as she smiled and headed to her
other table.

"Talk." Tabitha leaned back in
as her eyes sparkled.

"Calm down," said Summer with
a roll of her eyes as she put her
flute down.

"Don't be fucking jealous,
Summer, you'll get your turn,"

Tabitha said with an arched eyebrow, clicking the table with her long, hot pink fingernail like a naughty schoolteacher.

"Please," Summer said. She sat back with a playful pout at Tabitha.

Annie held her chuckle. The two were currently in a love-hate relationship with each other. Tabitha and Summer met the same man in the same night at different bars in downtown Cleveland—Heath.

Heath was hot as fuck. Annie remembered him well. He was a construction worker with rippling arm muscles that were barely contained in the tight blue T-shirt he had worn that night. His teal-colored eyes had been like shining jewels and his laugh had been contagious.

Once the two women found out they were into the same man, they decided that rather than ruin the friendship over a dick, they'd enjoy a threesome with him and that would be that. And it was. Or so Summer thought.

In truth, Tabitha had been sleeping with Heath off and on since that fateful night nine months ago. And Summer had been doing the same.

But the real catch was that she herself had given him her number, too. And for five solid months after that, she got to know the curve of his cock better than anyone at this table. But that was over now. For the best reasons possible. *I'm in love. Again.*

"You're quiet," Annie turned her attention to Fawn, the woman sitting next to Tabitha and the fourth woman who rounded out the weekly brunch club. Fawn had picked this week's spot in the Cleveland suburb of Lakewood, where the spring blossoms were in full bloom.

Some people described the five-foot, two-inches set designer as mousy, but Annie didn't think that was the right description. It wasn't mousy, it was understated. Fawn just preferred to be natural, with little make-up and her straight, dishwater blonde hair clean and short. Her eyes were hazel and clear, and when she looked at you, it was like she could see through you. She had a sensibility about herself and her approach to life that she refused to apologize for. Annie loved that.

"I'm interested," Fawn said. "Just tired."

"Was your husband's huge cock in your mouth all night?" Tabitha said with a teasing laugh.

"Lucky girl," Summer said. She leaned forward and gave Fawn a jesting smile.

For her part, Fawn just blushed and took a sip of coffee.

"Oh my God, did you really have his cock in your mouth all night?" Annie asked. This was the reason why "mousy" didn't fit Fawn. Fawn wasn't mousy. She was a firecracker in bed and her husband, Stanny, filled her pussy almost nightly with his huge cock. *Although last night, it seems it was in her mouth.*

"I love making him come," Fawn purred with a shrug.

The four women burst into laughter just as the waitress popped over again.

"You ladies ready to order?" she smiled.

"Just one little second, honey," Tabitha said.

"Sure," the waitress said as she breezed away.

"Fawn, you little slut," Tabitha said with admiration. "I bow to the fucking master."

"I know a good orthodontist in case your jaw can't take it anymore," Summer said. She would know. She sold various teeth tools and the men in her bed were usually dentists and doctors. It certainly explained her megawatt smile that she flashed now at Fawn along with a wink.

"Maybe some other time," Fawn said, turning her attention to Annie. "Today's story is about Annie's threesome."

"Yes," Tabitha said as her eyes turned to Annie with a renewed interest. "Did you eat pussy? Dick? Who was it with? How did it happen?"

Annie smiled as three sets of curious eyes turned her direction. She wished she had it in her to be a touch demurer like Fawn, but who was she kidding? She loved the attention.

"The only pussy that got eaten was mine," she said.

"The other girl didn't want oral?" Summer asked.

"There wasn't another girl," Annie responded.

"But that would mean…" Fawn started.

"Holy shit you had a threesome with two guys," Tabitha interrupted as she slapped a hand on the table.

"Two guys?" Summer asked. Annie could tell that her interest was genuine this time. "How did it happen? Who was it? Anyone we know?"

"Well, one of them you know," Annie said. Each of the girls leaned forward in anticipation. "My ex, the love of my life, the guy I was supposed to marry."

"Tommy?" Fawn asked, her eyes wide.

Annie nodded with a coy smile and the three girls collectively gasped in excited disbelief as they leaned back in varying stages of shock and pleasant surprise.

"Tommy? Hot Tommy?" Tabitha squealed. "His body is like Adonis."

"Yum," Summer said.

"And the other guy?" Fawn prodded.

"His boyfriend," Annie said.

Another chorus of gasps and varying levels and expressions of "No way!" erupted from the table.

"Tommy's gay?" Fawn asked.

"Bi," Annie replied.

"Did you know that?" Summer asked.

"I did. It never bothered me," Annie said. She shrugged with a sexy grin. "I thought it was hot. He'd tell me these stories about how he'd go down on a guy and make him come or how the sex was intense. It always made me hot."

"It is hot," Tabitha agreed.

"I'll decide if it's hot once I hear the story," said Summer.

Just then the waitress came back with a smile that was now barely concealing a look of annoyance.

"You ladies ready to order?"

"Yes," Annie said. "I'm starving. I'll take a stack of pancakes, one egg—"

"And two sausages," Tabitha said with a laugh.

"Two really big sausages," Fawn said with a wink.

"And keep the drinks coming," Summer added. "We're going to be here for a hot minute."

2

The Ex-Files

Tommy had been the brightest spot in Annie's day for more than three years. They had met on a plane while Annie was traveling to Italy for fun. Tommy was traveling there for a family reunion.

They were right across the aisle from each other and when she'd dropped her bag of peanuts (on purpose), his big, olive-colored hand picked it up and handed it to her. Their eyes had met and within one hour they had joined the mile-high club. They'd been inseparable after that, and the sex was the best she'd ever had.

"Your pussy is so wet," he'd groan in her ear as his thick cock would tightly rub every inch of her

12

insides including her G-spot, which he'd find and achingly caress until she was squirming.

"Fuck me harder," she'd moan. But he wouldn't. As soon as he knew she wanted it, loved it, needed more of it, he'd pull that monster out and slide the tip against her clit until her hips were circling in pleasure begging him to slide it back in.

"Mmm, how bad do you want this cock?" he had said to her many times, holding his cock and stroking that leaking tip against her sensitive, swollen folds.

"So bad," she'd yelled loud enough for her uptight neighbors to bang on the adjoining wall of their condo. "Fuck me. Please, fuck me."

And then he finally would. His rich, dark eyes would sparkle as his thick espresso-colored hair fell into his face courtesy of the powerful thrust of his cock deep inside her.

"More," she had screamed. And he'd given her more until he filled her with his salty release and collapsed on top of her. The weight of him had made her feel safe but it was always what he did next that made her feel loved.

He would gently take her lips in his and lightly kiss her as he whispered, "I love you so much."

"I love you, too," she had whispered back. *And God did I love him.*

He would kiss a trail down her neck, up to her ear, and take her earlobe in his mouth before lightly sucking it then moving to her cheek and back to her lips.

When she would let out a little whimper of pleasure, he'd roll on his side and bring her with him, tangling them up together in a figure eight as he would trail his fingertips lightly down her back.

"You're so sexy," he had said so
many times. She thought she would
never get tired of hearing that.
Especially from him. A bad boy.
The worst kind of bad boy with
Daddy's trust fund and an endless
supply of lovers. He had told her
that she had changed him and his
bad boy ways.

And in this very rare case, their
love actually had changed him. The
entire three years, two months, four
days, and ten hours they'd been a
couple, he had been faithful. Loyal.
He only had eyes for her, and he let
her know that. She could have
stayed in that relationship, just like
that, maybe forever.

But Tommy had wanted more.

"I can't believe this," he had said
in their cozy living room, holding
her platinum engagement ring in
his hand, the fire roaring behind
him on a freezing New Year's Day

in Cleveland. "I thought we both wanted this."

He had wanted to marry her, to have a baby with her, to use his millions to make sure she never had to work another day in her life if that's what she wanted. It almost killed her to see the pain in his eyes when she said, "I can't, Tommy."

"Don't you love me?"

"I do love you," she had said. "I'd live with you forever. The rest of my life, I swear to you. But…the marriage thing…I'm only 26, you're only 28…I'm not ready…it's not…"

She had trailed off at that point because there was nothing she could say in that moment that would make it easier for him. It was the ultimate rejection handed to him by someone he loved enough to buy a ring for. And for a bad boy like him, that was truly saying something.

"Tommy…"

"Don't," he'd said. He had put the ring back in its Tiffany box and set it on top of the fireplace. "I'll have my things moved out by next week."

And that had been it. He had quietly walked out the door. True to his word, a moving truck and Tommy arrived the next week.

She had watched as he packed all his things into boxes and the movers took them out. She hadn't been able to stop the tears and by the time he left, her eyes were devoid of make-up and the waste basket was filled to the brim with tissues.

He had stepped to her lightly and put those big hands around her face, lifting it up to his, and kissing her lips gently.

"I love you, Annie," he had whispered.

"I love you, too," she had choked out. She didn't want him to leave or for it to be over. But his pride wouldn't let him stay.

He had gently wiped her tears away then and kissed her on the forehead. He stepped back and took one more look around to see if he'd missed anything. That's when both of their gazes landed on the Tiffany's box still sitting on the fireplace.

She had quickly glanced to him to see what he would do next, but he just stared at it. It took a moment before he finally let out a sigh and turned a pained gaze back to her.

"It's your ring," he whispered.

"But…"

"It's yours, Annie."

He had reached down and trailed his index finger across her face with a sigh and kissed her again.

"Sell it if you'd like," he had said. "Or turn it into a necklace and wear it. Whatever you want."

"I can't do either of those things," she had whispered. And she had meant it. She couldn't sell it because she loved him. She couldn't wear it, in any form, because she wasn't ready to be married, and if she wore it, it would be like saying she was married, that she was his, forever and ever.

"Okay," he had said. She peered up at the man she loved and stared into those big, beautiful eyes. *Maybe someday one of us will change our mind.*

"I want to be married, Annie, and I want it to be you."

She hadn't been able to do or say anything except let the tears do her talking.

He left moments later. And she had spent the next several months staring at the Tiffany's box on the fireplace.

Then, on a random night out, all the girls met Heath and she thought he was a good idea for her broken heart. He meant nothing. He would never mean anything. And that's exactly what she needed.

Or so she thought.

3

Sex with the Ex

"Hey, Annie."

She would recognize Tommy's voice anywhere. It could be a crowded airport with jets flying overhead and she'd still be able to hear his voice and separate it from anyone else's. Every time she heard it, her heart would start to race.

True, she didn't say yes to his proposal. But she also didn't stop loving him.

"Tommy," she said in a breathy exhale.

It had been a full year since she turned him down. It was now another new year and she wasn't sure she could take yet another twelve months without him.

Hearing his voice only heightened that pain.

She had gone through six months of heartbreak after he left, then five months of Heath's big cock fucking her back to sanity, a month of sorting through the emotional mess still raging inside of her, and now, Tommy. Again. It was the first time they'd spoken since the horrible break-up that never truly felt like they had broken up, even though she knew he had been seeing some guy.

What could he possibly want now? Did they break up?

"How are you?" he asked. His voice was sweet, but tepid. She could tell he wanted to ask her something.

"I'm okay. You?"

She was surprised at herself that she wanted him to say he was terrible without her, too, that he missed her, that this guy meant nothing, that he wanted to talk. *But I said no. So, I don't get to want that.*

"I'm actually good," he said. His voice was filled with lightness, and she could tell he meant it. He *was* good. He was fucking better than she was.

"Oh," she said. Sensing her disappointment, he got straight to the point.

"I was wondering if we could talk," he half-said, half-asked. He sounded almost apologetic, and also a little hopeful.

"Sure," she said. "When?"

"Could I come over tonight? Maybe I could bring Chinese food and wine and we can catch up."

He knew her weaknesses. She, of course, wanted Chinese food and wine, and on top of all that, she, of course, wanted Tommy.

I want to see Tommy, but I don't want him. Wait, yes, I do. Do I? What is wrong with me?

"Sure, I'd like that," she said. Maybe a little too brightly.

"Great. I'll be over around 7."

"Sounds good," she said.

"Bye."

"Yeah, bye." She hung up the phone and looked at the fireplace. Something inside her ached a little. *What could he want? To get back together? To tell me he's moved on with this guy? What?*

She exhaled deeply then jumped up and headed to her bathroom.

If Tommy was showing up with Chinese food and wine at night, she was going to be ready. She hadn't slept with Heath in over a month and her monthly testing came back clean as a whistle. *It better be since I always use a condom.* Tommy was the same way about testing.

They both loved sex, but it had to be safe.

And now, it wasn't just about loving sex, but about love. *I hope.* And maybe, just maybe, if she could seduce him, she could win him back from this random guy, show him how much she wanted him, and he, in turn, would want her, too.

She had to be perfect for Tommy. Everything would be shaved, everything would be waxed, everything would be polished and made-up like she was about to fuck for her life.

Because in reality, I may very well be.

~~~
~~~

When Tommy knocked on the door, her heart lurched into her throat. She was smooth as silk from her head to her toes and wearing the short, red spaghetti-strap dress Tommy loved. It made her eyes shine a deep shade of green and accented her long, blonde locks perfectly as they tumbled over her soft, full breasts. Her heels were the strappy ones, the ones he made her leave on while he held her ankles and slid deep inside her wetness.

"Hi," she said as she opened the door to her—*our*—condo.

"Wow," he said. He stood there holding the wine and food while he generously surveyed every inch of her body. She took a deep breath to push her breasts higher and delighted at his stare when it rested on them as they heaved.

She peered down to his dark jeans, which fit him perfectly, and could see he was already getting hard just from looking at her. When his eyes dipped down to her heels, his firmness turned rock hard.

"Annie," he barely croaked out before she brazenly grabbed both sides of his face with her hands and deeply kissed him. *Oh my God, what am I doing?*

He didn't stop her. Instead, he reached down and slid his biceps under her hips and lifted her to him, spreading her legs and pushing her aching folds against his black sweater.

"Tommy," she panted.

"Fuck, Annie," he said. He was barely holding it together as he carried her through the door, dropped the food and wine on the carpet and slammed the door shut. He started using his big hands to move her dress up over her hips until it gathered at her lower back and stomach.

"Fuck, no panties," he said as he grabbed her ass and squeezed it, pulling on it and making her holes spread eagerly.

"Open me up, baby," she said as he carried her into the living room and sat her down onto the couch.

"Annie, wait, I'm with someone—"

"Stop, Tommy," she interrupted. "You're mine. Always."

And she believed that. It didn't matter who else there was, there would always be a Tommy and Annie. And that was never going to change.

And Tommy apparently agreed.

"Spread your legs," he said roughly. And she did, opening them wide so he could gaze deeply at everything between them. His sultry stare made every single private place blossom and engorge with pleasure under his spell.

"Take me, Tommy," she panted, pulsing her hips into the air, begging for his cock.

He smiled then and she remembered all the times he'd made her beg. He loved to tease her, slowly and easily until she could barely stand it. And that's what he did now.

"Not yet," he breathed. He grabbed her ankles and spread her legs even more making her gasp with pleasure. He ran his hands down the back of her legs with a strong pressure that made her moan.

"Oh God, Tommy, yes," she whimpered. She arched her back against the couch, her mouth open with desire as his hands reached her pleasure zone and spread her even wider from either side. He rolled her sensitive skin in his hands to make her open and close, open and close, open and close. It made a delicious smacking noise that told them both how wet she was.

"Oh God," she moaned. She looked down into his eyes as they stared right at her. He smiled knowing how much she loved this.

"Take me in your mouth, Tommy," she ordered. She reached down and grabbed his hair, nudging him toward her.

"Whatever you want, beautiful," he said. He leaned down between her legs and took a deep breath. "God, you smell amazing."

"Fuck," she whimpered with pleasure.

Just then, he launched his tongue into her lips, finding her clit and slowly sucking on it, then licking around it, then sucking, then licking, sucking, licking.

"More," she ordered.

He moved down her slit and plunged his tongue deep inside her,

French kissing her pussy with urgency and desire.

"Tommy, yes," she moaned. "Yes, please, more."

And he gave her more, moving from her pussy to the tightest hole on her body. The one he loved best. His tongue slowly traced the outside of it with his tongue as she squirmed under its spell.

"Lick my ass more," she shuddered as pleasure tingled all over her body.

He changed pressures moving from the tip of his tongue teasing the hole, to a hard pressure from his whole tongue as he kissed it.

"I'm gonna come," she moaned.

"Come, baby," he said. He jabbed his tongue deep inside her tight ass and massaged her with it until waves of pleasure moved through her body.

"I'm coming so hard," she moaned. The waves tightened her

stomach with a glorious sensation that didn't stop for several seconds. "Fuck."

She gripped his hair and moved it in time with the orgasm that was ravaging her body with a pleasure only Tommy could give her. When she finally relaxed and let go of his dark mane, she peered down into an intense stare.

"Fuck me, Tommy," she moaned.

"How deep?" he asked as he wiped his mouth. He pulled off his sweater revealing his beautiful, rippling chest. He stood up between her legs. She could see how hard he was through his jeans as he slowly unbuttoned them and released the monster from its cage. She gasped with pleasure.

"Sink it deep in me, baby," she breathed.

He pulled off every last stitch of his clothing and spread her legs even further as she reached up and stroked him. He moaned at her touch, then grabbed her wrists and asked with heightened pleasure, "Is the lube in the same place?"

She smiled. "Of course."

He smiled and rubbed down her arms, before walking away. "I'll be right back."

"I'll be waiting," she said. She loved that he knew where everything was, that he knew how to please her, that he just *knew* her. She brought her legs down and reached between them to keep the pleasure going. She glanced back at the fireplace.

This isn't why he came, but, damn it, it'll be the reason he stays if it's the last thing I do.

4

Deep Inside You

By the time Tommy came back, she was soaking wet and ready for him to plunge deep inside her.

"Tommy," she said with an urgency she hadn't had for any man other than him.

"Annie," he said as he watched her rub her pussy with those intense, dark eyes.

"You're so beautiful," he said with a controlled hunger as his eyes drank in her spread legs, her tight, pink pussy, the ass that was already open for him. "God, I want you."

"Take me," she moaned.

He grabbed her around her tiny waist with both hands and lifted her off the couch in one strong movement.

"Baby," she gasped. He carried
her down the hallway and back to
the bedroom. She could smell mint
on his breath. *He brushed his teeth.
So, he can kiss me while he's deep
inside me.*

She couldn't wait for him to do
it, so she lightly touched her lips to
his to let him know she wanted it as
much as he did. He took the hint
and moaned as he opened his
mouth, dipping his tongue between
her lips over and over again with a
passion they both remembered
well.

She was wet and throbbing by
the time he laid her down on the
King-sized bed, still kissing her as
he spread her legs and settled
between them on his knees. His
cock was stiff and at the ready.

"Take me, Tommy," she moaned
as he released her from their kiss.

"Yes," he moaned. "God, yes."

He slowly inserted the tip into her wet pussy causing them both to moan loudly.

"It feels so good," he choked out. He put his hands on the backs of her knees and spread her legs wider to accommodate his thickness.

"Tommy, yes, slide it in," she moaned, tipping her hips up to take the whole thing in as he moved his hands down the back of her thighs and spread her even wider. It drove her crazy the way he opened her up. "Put it all in, baby, please!"

She was squirming now underneath him lifting her hips and pushing him deeper by sliding onto his cock. She could see the pleasure on his face as his lips parted and he pushed against her to sink his cock even further.

They both moaned with an unbearable pleasure.

"Annie," he choked as he pushed deeper and deeper.

"Yes, Tommy, yes," she panted. They pushed against each other to drive him deeper and deeper until the monster was all the way in. He buried his cock in her wet pussy, as it throbbed against her sensitive skin.

"Holy shit," he moaned. "I'm so deep inside you, Annie. Fuck."

"Fuck me, baby," she cried out. He started to slowly pulse his hips and drive his cock against her insides. His balls were slamming against her ass making it tingle with pleasure as he drove and drove and drove that solid dick into her wetness.

"Oh, Annie, fuck," he moaned as he let go of her thighs and grabbed the tiny spaghetti straps of her red dress and snapped them like twigs, her breasts bouncing out and joining in the fun.

"Yes!" she gasped with pleasure as a smile erupted across her face. Tommy was the best lover she'd ever had, and this was why. He knew how to be soft and hard, how to be a gentleman and how to be a savage, and just when to do all of it with the ease of a lover who knew what he was doing.

"Hold me down!" she yelled. He complied, grabbing each of her wrists with each of his hands and slamming them behind her head. He held her down and dropped his weight onto her so his chest was achingly rubbing against her nipples. Every erogenous zone was being touched, banged, and rubbed by his body. "Tommy, make me come!"

"Annie, yes," he groaned. His hips pumped harder and faster, owning her the way he used to. *The way I still want him to.*

"That's it, Tommy, right there, baby," she said. She joined his rhythm with her own body, banging against him, her body hungry for every sweaty, delicious piece of him.

"Annie, I'm gonna come, baby," he choked out as she saw that look come across his face. The look she was so familiar with. He would close his eyes and part his lips as his strong, beautiful body would become unhinged and bang her like his life depended on it. He was ready to come, and she wanted him, all of him, inside her. He was the only man she would let do such a thing. He was the only man she trusted for that kind of intimate act.

"Come inside me, baby," she demanded as she took his cock even deeper with her hips.

"Yes, God, yes, I wanna fill you up," he moaned.

"Yes, Tommy, yes," she said as she squirmed underneath him. "Fill me!"

And he did. On their bed, in their home, together like they always had been, him coming inside her, loving her, with the hope for a future together. *And I do want a future with Tommy. I can't believe it. I want it. I want it.*

She came so hard, she could barely breathe as he shakily finished filling her up. He slowly lowered himself on top of her and did the thing he always used to—kissing her gently and saying those words.

"I still love you, Annie," he said gently as his breath slowed.

"I still love you, too, Tommy," she said quietly as she got her breathing under control. "I never stopped."

"Me either," he said. He gave her a slightly guilty look and rolled over onto his back. "Fuck, Annie."

"What?" Now she was confused as the heat of the moment and the love that passed between seemed to momentarily cool. "Tommy, what?"

"I couldn't help myself with you," he said. He rubbed his temples and then looked at her. "I came over here to ask…"

"Ask what?" She could feel a sinking feeling in her stomach. *That's right, he called for something. He had a reason for coming over. Is it the guy?* "Tell me, Tommy. Why did you want to see me if not for this?"

He looked at the ceiling as though there was something terribly interesting there. He finally looked at her.

"The relationship I'm in," he said. "It's serious, Annie."

As soon as he said it, it felt like a kick to the stomach. "Oh."

She jumped up and pulled her destroyed dress off her body. She grabbed at the first pair of comfy joggers she could find and a plain, white tank top, throwing them on with force as she whipped back to him.

"I let you come in me," she said, the tears brimming in her eyes. "I thought this was real, that you missed me—"

"I do fucking miss you," he said as he stood, his nakedness beautiful, solid, and strong. "Annie. I still love you. I wanted everything that happened here tonight. I came over because I wanted to see if you still wanted me, too. I thought we might get to talk first."

They both half-laughed at the absurdity they could ever keep their hands off each other.

"But as soon as I saw you…I couldn't stop. I love you too damn much. Want you too damn much."

Her eyes softened. He was right. She hadn't realized how badly she wanted it, too. How badly she wanted him. Neither one of them could have stopped that freight train.

And she should have asked him the basic question: Who is the guy all over your Instagram account? She blew right by it in favor of capturing his heart back. It was his fault and her fault. They both leaped without looking.

"So, who is he? How serious is it?" she asked.

"His name is Christopher," he said gently. "I love him. We're living together."

She couldn't help the tears that pricked at her eyes. "Then why are you here for me?"

"Christopher knows how much I love you, how I wanted to marry you, and he—"

"He what?" she interruped. She felt disappointment begin to rise in her chest again.

"He told me I should see…should try one last time, to get you back. To see if you wanted to join us," he said sheepishly.

"Join you?" she asked, confused. "Join you how?"

"Join us in every way," Tommy said quietly as his intense eyes held her stare. "Annie, my love for you…it's never going to go away. It never has. It never will. You changed me. You're why I could love Christopher. Why I could never go back to my bad habits. You. And the way you looked at me tonight, the way you let me take you…I think you feel the same way."

She couldn't speak as he took a step toward her and reached his hand out to touch her face.

"I love you so much. But, I love Christopher, too. And I don't think I can live without either of you."

"Tommy," she whispered as she leaned her face into his hand. She had never entertained such a notion. *A throuple situation? Seriously? No.*

She took in his dark eyes and all she could feel was love. That same, big love she'd always felt when it came to Tommy. *Maybe.*

"I don't know, Tommy," she whispered.

"That's not a no," he whispered back.

He stepped closer and leaned his naked body into her, dropping his mouth onto hers and kissing her deeply. She moved onto her tippy toes and pushed for his tongue deeper and deeper until they were both panting from a desire only they shared.

She pulled away and stared into his eyes. "I'll meet him," she whispered.

Tommy smiled broadly and lightly kissed her again. "That's all I ask."

He deeply kissed her one last time before pulling back and gazing at her face. "And Annie?"

"Yeah?"

"Don't think I didn't see the ring still on the fireplace."

She gasped. She had never touched the ring. She'd only seen it when Tommy opened the box. After he shut it, she'd never looked again. It was in the exact same place he had left it. The box dusty. The ribbon slightly yellowed.

"I think that means something," he whispered.

"It does," she acknowledged. "But, Tommy—"

"Just meet him, Annie," he interrupted. "And then, we can see how it goes from there, okay? I promise. I'll be careful with your heart."

He pulled her into a hug, and she closed her eyes against his tight chest. *I hope you will be.*

5

The Boyfriend

As soon as Annie laid eyes on Christopher in the busy café on the west side of Cleveland, she felt an attraction. He was tall like Tommy, more than six feet, and he was wearing expensive clothing that fit him perfectly. The blue sweater stretched provocatively across his muscled chest down to his dark jeans and dress boots.

"Hi," he said with a touch of heat. He drank in her tight figure and large breasts. They were barely caged in a button-down cream-colored sweater that fell just at her taut waist. Her fitted blue jeans stretched nicely over her Pilates ass. "Wow."

She smiled and tossed her long, blonde hair as she reveled in the pleasure across his face. "You, too," she said coyly.

He stepped into her and whispered, "I hope I'm not being too forward." He slowly pulled her into a hug, wrapping his strong arms around her as she pushed her body into his and hugged him back.

"Not too forward at all," she whispered into his ear as she rubbed her nipples against him. She could feel his cock start to harden against her pussy and was pleased to feel it was thick and long, just like she liked.

"Mmm," she moaned lightly as he let out a quiet grunt in her ear.

"Fuck," he breathed. He pulled back just a little so he could gaze into her eyes. His breath was on her lips. "Tommy was right about you."

She grinned with pleasure at him. "I'll take that as a compliment."

"Meant as one." His eyes moved from her face down to her plush breasts and back to her eyes. "Beautiful."

"Hey now," said Tommy. He stepped to Annie as Christopher slowly backed away and Tommy moved in. As one backed off and the other came in, they paused to gaze at each other before Christopher leaned in and took Tommy's lips in his own with a slight sucking and then a quick kiss.

Annie gasped at the site. Not because it was two men, not because it was Tommy, but because of how turned on she immediately became at seeing the passion between them. *God, I'm so wet.*

"Mmm," moaned Christopher. "I could do that all day."

"I wouldn't stop you," said Tommy. Annie could see he was pleased at the attention, giving Christopher a playful slap on the ass as Tommy moved in to hug Annie and Christopher slid back into the booth.

"Hi beautiful," Tommy whispered as his gaze landed on Annie's face. He gently kissed her lips and she could feel her pussy start to swell and throb with desire. "Your nipples are hard."

Without anyone seeing, he reached his hand up and brushed his thumb in a steady motion across one of her nipples.

"Tommy," she whispered with pleasure.

"You like that?" he whispered in her ear as he achingly rubbed her nipple.

"Fuck yes," she quietly moaned.

"There's more where that came from," he said. He stopped the motion and gave her a quick peck on the lips before grabbing her hand and guiding her into the booth on his side of the table.

As she slid in, she could feel the wetness starting to come through her panties. *Holy shit I want them both inside of me.*

She peered across the table at Christopher, who had the same look of desire, and heard Tommy chuckle beside her. She glanced at him. "What?"

"I don't think sexual chemistry is going to be an issue," he said quietly as he slid his hand between her crossed legs and slowly rubbed the inside of her thigh near her pussy.

"Tommy," she whispered in a husky voice.

"Don't stop on my account," Christopher whispered from the table. When she opened her eyes, he was hotly staring at her, so she returned the gaze.

"Okay," said Tommy, breaking the heat. He pulled his hand from between her legs and put his big hands gently on the table. "Okay. Let's hit the pause button. And maybe, I don't know, take some time to get to know each other a little bit. I'm sure you have questions."

Tommy looked directly at Annie and she was reminded of the first year they dated. Tommy had led the relationship, always stopping and asking questions, checking in on her feelings, taking "status checks," he would say, of where they were. At first, she thought it was really stupid. She was wild and passionate and led with her heart. And Tommy felt like a downer, who was supposed to be a wild, bad boy.

"Stop that shit," she had said that first year. And he had looked hurt when she did.

"I love you, Annie," he had said. "I've never been in love before. And this is how I do it."

And once he had said that she shut right the fuck up. She let him lead. She let him take "status checks" and soon enough, she realized it was actually helpful. When she couldn't find the words or didn't know how to approach a conversation, Tommy would pop up with a "status check," and she could say the thing she needed to.

That's what he was doing now. Slowing it down. Taking a status check. Letting everyone say what they needed to say. Letting her ask what she needed to ask. Not because he didn't have the same desire. *I can see his hard cock in those jeans.* But because his desire to merge his two worlds in a meaningful way was stronger than his desire to just fuck them both. He'd done that for all his life before he met her. And she knew he was done with all that.

"I think I do have questions," she said as Christopher and Tommy both smiled at her. She relaxed and they did, too. In that moment, she felt like she could breathe again. A delicate laugh escaped her lips and they followed suit, the sexual tension downgrading from a category five hurricane to a tropical storm.

"Ask anything you want," Christopher said. And now, in the calm, she could see kindness and warmth behind his blue eyes. The way he took care of himself, with his dark blonde hair carefully sculpted in a wave away from his face, that showed off his chiseled features. To be honest, he looked like a movie star.

"Are you a model or something?" she asked.

"God, I wish," Christopher said with a laugh. "I'm an architect. I own my own firm."

"You own your own firm? You're so young."

"I'm very good at my job," he said. "And I love it. I've wanted to do it since I was a kid."

"Really?"

"Really," he said with a smile. *God, that smile makes me melt a little.* "It started with building blocks as a child and went from there."

Just then the waiter stopped at the table and gave his attention to Annie.

"Drink, Miss?"

"A mimosa," she said sweetly as the waiter nodded.

"Your I.D., Miss," he said almost apologetically.

"God bless you," she said with a laugh. Tommy winked at her as she reached for her phone and pulled her driver's license out of the case.

"Thank you," the waiter said as he handed her back her license and walked away.

"Tommy said you're 27?"

"I am," she said. She put her license back and set her phone down. "And you are?"

"I'm 31," he said.

"Older man," she said with a sly smile. She peered at Tommy and gave him a seductive wink as a light blush spread across his cheeks.

"Indeed," Tommy said with an arched eyebrow. "Only by two years, though."

"Older is older," Christopher said as he took a sip of his whiskey. "Annie, Tommy said you're a party planner?"

"That's how we met," she said. And she couldn't help the tears that stung her eyes right then as she glanced at Tommy with adoration. She could feel that big love from her head to heart and all the way down to her toes.

"Annie," Tommy whispered. He leaned over and kissed her gently as she pulled herself together.

"I'm sorry," she said quietly.

"It's okay," he whispered. He put his hand on her thigh and gave her a gentle squeeze. "We can go. It's okay. Really. This was too much."

"No," she said. She took a deep breath and sat up straight to look into his eyes. "Tommy, I love you. I want to be with you. And if you love Christopher, then I want to know him."

And now Tommy was the one to go silent as his eyes misted over and he gazed at her lovingly.

"That's how I feel about you, too, Annie," Christopher said quietly.

She turned and gazed into Christopher's loving eyes.

"I know how much Tommy loves you. And I would never keep him from you. Never. Even if you and I didn't hit it off. If we couldn't be a throuple. I would never stop him from still being with you."

She nodded at him with a smile. She wasn't sure what to say to Chris or Tommy, but she knew that saying it in a public place didn't feel like something she wanted to do right now. There were a lot of emotions, more than she could handle anyone else seeing right now.

"Let's go somewhere more private," she said quietly.

"Okay," Tommy said.

"Of course," Christopher agreed. He caught the waiter's attention and made a signal for the check. "Where would you like to go?"

That was easy. She needed to be somewhere that made her feel safe.

"Home base," she said with a shaky smile as she glanced at Tommy. "Our home."

6

You Show Me Yours

As soon as the door of their condo shut, Annie could feel the sexual tension make a hasty return. She couldn't stop herself from turning to Tommy and sliding her hands up his chest.

"Annie," he whispered. His hands found her breasts and rubbed them deliciously slow, thumbing her nipples and making them stand at attention.

"Yes," she panted as his cock hardened against her. She peered around him at Christopher, who looked hungry to take them both. "I want to see you two together."

"What?" Tommy pulled back in surprise. "What do you mean? Like, you want to watch?"

She nodded as she gave Christopher a heated look that made him swell even more than he already was.

"Tommy, if you want me to seriously consider this thing." she said, eyeing him, "Then I want to see you two make love. I want to know the way you feel about each other. How you please each other. To see if—"

"There's any room for you?" Tommy asked. There he went again, knowing her better than she knew herself sometimes. And right now, he knew she didn't want to reveal herself, her vulnerabilities, without seeing his.

If Tommy loved Christopher enough to not let him go, even for her, then she wanted to see, to know, what that looked like, so that she could know how she might fit into this three-part relationship equation.

"Yes," she said quietly.

"I'll do anything you want, baby," Tommy said as he looked to Christopher.

For his part, Christopher simply smiled with a sexy stare at Tommy, and then Annie. She could see he wasn't offended, just thinking. About what, she couldn't decipher.

"What?" she asked. He raked his sultry stare over her entire body making her pussy respond with a wet heat.

"I'm happy to make love to Tommy in front of you and let you into our relationship," he said. "But…"

He flicked an arched eyebrow at her, half as a challenge, half as a nod to the fact that he felt vulnerable in this scenario, too. "I want the same in return."

That's when it really hit her. *Oh shit, we're both in love with the same man. We're both feeling this insecurity about the other.*

She nodded at him. "That's fair," she said. "You can watch us, too."

"Okay," he said quietly. She could see his eyes soften a little. He knew she was going to give a little, too, to make him as comfortable as he was trying to make her feel comfortable. *Maybe this could work?*

Christopher slowly walked over to her, and she appreciated his panther-like gait as he stopped right in front of her. He whispered, "Feel free to make yourself come when we do."

She couldn't stop the light moan that escaped her lips as Christopher turned to Tommy and slid his big hands under Tommy's sweater. He dragged them up and down Tommy's back before landing a deep, passionate kiss on Tommy's lips.

"Holy shit," she whispered. She felt her pussy swell and engorge as she watched Christopher's hand slide down Tommy's back and onto his taut ass. He gripped it and massaged it until Tommy moaned with pleasure.

"Chris," Tommy whispered as Christopher released Tommy's mouth and moved slowly down his neck before he stepped away.

"Where's the bedroom, baby?" Christopher asked Tommy.

"I'll show you," Annie half-panted. She was going to get a prime seat in the oversized chair near the bed and use her vibrator while she watched them together. *It's too hot not to.*

"Let's go," Tommy said. He grabbed Christopher's hand with a smile and led him down the hallway behind Annie.

"Your ass is so beautiful, baby," Tommy said to Annie.

She flicked him a quick smile over her shoulder. "Thanks, baby."

When they got to the bedroom, Annie walked past the bed to the chair, opened the nightstand next to it and grabbed her bullet massager. She turned to watch Christopher peel off his sweater and gasped at his chest. He was a perfectly chiseled specimen of man, smooth and hairless, his nipples hard and ready for Tommy's mouth.

He stepped to Tommy and helped Tommy wiggle out of his sweater, throwing it on the floor and kneeling in front of Tommy.

"I want you so bad," Christopher whispered. He kissed Tommy's stomach right above his belt as he unbuckled it, then slowly loosened the button and unzipped Tommy's jeans.

"Yes," Tommy whispered. He sunk his hands deep into those gentle waves of dark blonde hair as

Christopher slowly pulled down Tommy's jeans and underwear, revealing his thick, rock-hard cock.

"Oh, yes," Christopher whispered as he helped Tommy step out of his shoes, socks, and clothing. Then he gently and slowly started to put Tommy's cock in his mouth.

"Oh," Tommy moaned as he guided Christopher's mouth, gripping his hair with pleasure.

Holy shit. I might come just watching.

Annie had to catch her breath watching them. She could see immediately that this was love. It was hot sex, of course, but it was underscored with love and a desire to please the other. *Beautiful.*

That's when Tommy looked at her, like he knew she was thinking about him. The pleasure on his face soaked her panties.

"Take your clothes off, Annie," he said, barely getting it out as Christopher slowly and achingly worked Tommy's cock down his throat. "Oh, Chris, take me deeper in your mouth."

She watched with delight, stripping down to nothing, as Christopher took all of Tommy deep in his throat and sucked and swallowed until Tommy nearly came undone in his mouth. Just as he almost lost it, Christopher stopped and pulled back, smiling up at Tommy, who whimpered at his stopping.

"Not yet, baby," Christopher said as he stood up. "Don't come until I'm deep inside you."

"Chris," Tommy whimpered. He pulled Chris into a passionate kiss, helping him take his pants off, too.

Annie stopped rubbing her naked pussy long enough to gasp at Christopher's throbbing giant. It wasn't as long as Tommy's, but it was thicker. The kind of cock that could make you scream just from entering you.

"I want it," Annie whispered to herself as she started touching herself again. *Take him, Christopher. Make him come hard.*

"Lay down," Christopher ordered Tommy.

"Yes, baby," Tommy said. He scooted back on the bed and spread his legs for Christopher. "I want you so bad."

"I want you, too," Christopher said. He grabbed Tommy by the hips and pulled him to the edge of the bed before dropping to his knees. "I wanna taste you."

"Yes," Tommy moaned. "Open me up. Eat me until I'm ready for you."

Annie flicked on her vibrator, pressing it against her clit, starting to pant as she watched Christopher gently lick Tommy's balls and take them lightly into his mouth, making Tommy groan with pleasure.

"Your mouth feels so good on my balls," Tommy panted. "More, please, baby."

Christopher obliged, moving down, down, down, until the tip of his tongue was teasing Tommy's tight hole.

"Baby, yes!" Tommy was writhing now under Christopher's sexy mouth and Annie was about to lose it as her orgasm started to slowly build. *They're so hot and sexy together.*

Tommy gasped loudly as Christopher buried his tongue into his ass, French kissing it and making Tommy grab the covers into tight balls in his fists.

"Chris!" Tommy screamed. "Baby, slide your cock in me."

Christopher lifted his head with a heady look at Annie. "Lube?"

"Drawer," she panted. She nodded at the nightstand by the bed, barely able to speak as she felt her orgasm take the stage.

Christopher moved stealthily to the drawer. He grabbed the lube and came back with it already open, his cock wet with it. He dripped a little more onto his fingertips and slowly started to massage Tommy's ass as Tommy spread his legs wider.

"Yes, baby, yes," Tommy moaned. "Get me ready for you."

"Yes," Christopher panted as he slowly slid one finger, then two, into Tommy, opening him up as they both looked ready to explode with pleasure.

"Take me, baby," Tommy moaned. "Please, take me."

Seeing Tommy beg Christopher for his cock, the way she would beg Tommy for *his* cock, was perhaps the most intoxicating thing she'd ever seen. *He's submissive in their relationship.*

"Take his cock, Tommy," she whispered. She upped her vibrator speed and could feel her orgasm gather.

Christopher slowly edged his thick cock inside of Tommy. First the tip as Tommy moaned with pleasure.

"Holy shit, yes," Tommy panted. "More, please, more."

"Whatever you want, baby," Christopher moaned as he pushed gently deeper and deeper, his face warping into pleasure. "You're so tight. You make me wanna come right now."

"Baby, come in me," Tommy whimpered.

"Fuck," Christopher said as he slid all the way inside Tommy. "I'm balls deep, baby. You're so tight."

"Oh, fuck," Tommy screamed with pleasure. "You're so deep. It feels so fucking good."

"I'm gonna slow fuck you baby until you come," Christopher panted.

Oh, shit, I'm about to come. Annie pulsed her hips as Christopher rocked his cock into Tommy, both of them moaning in pleasure as their orgasms ratcheted up.

"Yes, baby, I'm gonna come," Tommy screamed.

"I'm coming, baby, I'm coming," Christopher moaned.

"Come inside me," Tommy panted.

"Yes, yes!" Christopher panted. "I'm coming!"

Christopher pushed one final powerful thrust into Tommy and stayed there pulsing while they both came. Annie felt her orgasm rise and explode inside of her. She could barely stay put in the chair she came so hard. *That was so hot.*

But it was what happened next that had the most effect on Annie. When she finished coming and looked at the two men together, they were wrapped together in a figure eight. Tommy whispered, "I love you so much."

"I love you, too, baby. You're so beautiful," Christopher said back.

It was a beautiful moment. And one she would never want to steal from Tommy.

I have to give this a shot. A real one. For Tommy. And for the love he and I still share.

7

And I'll Show You Mine

As Annie took in the love between the two men, she felt a sudden and deep connection to Christopher. She didn't know him, true, but she didn't need to for her to understand that she and him, they were the same.

We both love Tommy. And loving Tommy and having him love you back was something truly special. Annie was the first member to join that club. Christopher was the second. It was a unique experience and one you cherished every second you were in it.

"Annie?"

She snapped back to attention to find them both looking at her, pleasure all over their faces, staring

sexily at her, waiting for her next
move.

"Sorry," she said. She sat up and
smiled at them. "You two are really
amazing together."

They both nodded.

"There's room for you, Annie,"
said Tommy. "I promise."

Christopher smiled warmly at
her. "You can see how much I love
him?"

"Yeah," she said. "I can."

Christopher smiled, then slowly
rose from the bed and stood as
Tommy rubbed his foot against
Chris's thigh with a satisfied smile.
Chris reached out his hand to
Annie.

"Shower with us?" he asked.

Her heart lurched a little. She
wasn't quite sure she was ready to
be with them both just yet, but she
also didn't want to say no. She
could try and deny it all she
wanted, but she was attracted to

Chris. She already knew that she wanted to feel him deep inside her.

"Sure," she said with a shrug. "But no funny business. Yet."

Chris smiled at her playful warning and accepted her boundaries. "Of course," he said. "You're in control of this."

"Thank you," she said. She took his hand and led him to the bathroom. She heard Tommy slide off the bed and follow them.

The bathroom was attached to the master bedroom. Tommy had done that when they first bought the condo. He hired contractors and broke a few walls, added some streaked marble, upgraded all the gadgets, and made this her most favorite room in the whole place.

There were three nozzles in three separate places on the shower walls, and one waterfall head on the ceiling. There were places to sit and fuck, and no shower door. She and Tommy had made love multiple times in this shower and something on Chris's face as they stepped into it told her that he already knew that.

"Did Tommy tell you how much I love this shower?" she asked coyly. He just smiled and turned on the hot water from all four nozzles until it was steamy and warm. She felt her muscles relax as the water wet her body with strong streams. She took pleasure in Christopher watching every inch of her.

"You're incredibly sexy," he said.

"Mmm," she moaned as she lathered her breasts with soap, enjoying the tingling sensation when her fingers brushed the hardened tips as Chris watched.

Tommy stepped into the shower then and already his cock was hard. "Annie," he panted. He wrapped his hand around his huge cock and pleasured himself as he watched her rinse the soap away. She pinched her nipples and then followed the water with her fingers to her clit, rubbing it as she stared into Tommy's eyes.

"Take me, Tommy," she said headily. She could barely focus as Tommy moved quickly to her and took her mouth into a passionate kiss while sliding two fingers between her legs and making her insides slick. "Yes!"

"Annie, you're so wet," he panted. "So, beautiful."

The water rushed over both of them as Tommy fingered her deeply. He added another thick digit to make her hips squirm with pleasure, as she rode his hand like it was his huge manhood.

"Tommy!" she moaned. "Slide your cock in me."

"Not yet," he said. He released her and led her to one of the seats in the shower.

"Sit down, baby," he ordered.

"Yes, Tommy," she said submissively. She gave him a sexy smile.

"Mmm, that's right, baby," he said. "Now, spread your legs."

She did as she was told and watched with delight as he dipped to his knees and buried his face between her legs. It was then that she peered over to Chris, who was stroking his own cock as he watched Tommy.

"Eat my pussy, baby," she moaned, catching Chris' stare and holding it while they both panted with pleasure. "More, Tommy, more."

She broke Chris' stare as the pleasure overtook her and she felt her orgasm start to tingle in her pelvis. She grabbed Tommy's hair and pulled it to make him look at her. "I want you inside me, baby. In my ass."

"Annie," he panted. "Yes."

He stood and walked out of the shower, touching Chris' chest as he breezed out. He returned just a split second later with the lube, his cock already shiny with it.

"Let me get you ready, baby," he said.

She stood and turned around, getting on her knees on the shower seat and lifting her ass in the air toward Tommy. "I want you so bad, Tommy."

"Baby," he said as his breath caught. "Your perfect ass is so tight and pink."

"I want you inside it," she whimpered. She moved it up and down, opening her tight hole as much as she could for him, which turned them both on.

"Yes, baby, yes," he moaned. He took his lubed-up fingers and slowly started massaging her tight, pink hole as it opened a little bit at a time.

"Tommy, yes!" She could feel her ass opening for him and all she wanted was for him to slide it in and fill her up. "Fill me, baby."

"Yes, baby," he said. He took hold of his cock and slowly pushed the tip in.

"Baby!" she moaned. She caught Chris's stare and saw that his orgasm was starting to bloom as well. His face was a beautiful shade of pleasure.

"Annie, fuck," Tommy moaned. He slowly kept sliding deeper and deeper as she pushed against him and gently took him in.

"Tommy, yes, baby, more, slowly," she panted. They rocked back and forth like that until he gave one final push and she almost came just from feeling his huge cock fill her ass with its thickness.

"Annie, baby, fuck, I'm all the way in," he moaned. He started pulsing lightly as she squirmed around his cock, moaning.

"Tommy, it feels so fucking good." And it did. She could barely contain herself with him inside of her like that. "Harder, baby, harder."

"Yes, baby," he said. He started to rock against her harder.

"Baby, I can feel your balls against my clit," she yelled. "Harder, make me come."

"Like that?" he asked as he pulled her hips up higher and rocked against her, banging her clit hard with his big balls.

"Tommy!" she screamed. "Yes! Fuck me!"

And he did, fucking her ass with abandon as they wildly drove each other to the edge. Just as she was about to come, she locked eyes with Chris.

"I'm coming!" she screamed. Chris orgasmed, too, in huge powerful squirts of come all over their shower floor. Every time he squirted out his release, she felt a powerful surge in her pussy.

"I'm coming," Tommy yelled. He gripped her hips and thrust deep inside her.

"Come in me, baby," she said with urgency. Tommy rocked against her, his cock so deep she swore she could feel it in her throat.

"I'm filling you with my come, baby," he grunted as he pulsed and pushed his come deep inside her.

"That's it, baby," she cooed as she looked at Tommy over her shoulder. "Yes, baby."

"Annie," he said breathily as he caught her stare and held it as he finished.

She smiled at him seductively as he finished. He slowly pulled out of her and gently pulled her to her feet, wrapping her in his strong arms. He kissed her lips gently.

"I love you so much, Annie," he said, smiling at her.

"I love you, too, Tommy," she said gently.

"Did I hurt you?"

"No," she smiled. "That was amazing, baby."

"Good," he grinned. "Annie, this thing…I don't ever want to hurt you. Or do anything that would make you feel like I didn't love you. We can stop. Anytime."

"I know," she whispered. She glanced over at Chris and smiled. He smiled back at her as he rinsed himself off. She looked deeply into Tommy's eyes. "I want to try it."

"Really?" he asked.

She nodded.

"Annie, don't do it because you think you might lose me. You won't. Either way."

"He's right," Chris said. He stepped toward them. "Annie, you don't have to become a throuple. I'm open to this relationship in any form. Even if it means I might only have Tommy as a friend. I mean that. You're in total control here. I can see how much you two love each other. Want each other. I won't step between you two if you only want Tommy."

"Chris—" Tommy started.

"Tommy. She's your girl. I can see that. I want you both to be happy."

Chris turned to leave and as he did, Annie was surprised that she reached out and grabbed his arm. "Wait."

Chris turned around and they both looked at her in surprise.

"What if the possibility exists that I might want you both? Tommy? Would you be okay with that?"

Tommy's stare turned serious as he thought through what she was saying. That was Tommy. To seriously consider everything, and be thoughtful about it. "So, a relationship between all three of us?" he asked her. "Not just me and you, and then me and Chris, but rather, all three in one relationship with each other?"

She nodded as she eyed Chris, who was seductively eyeing her body. "Chris?" she asked.

"I think you're incredibly sexy, Annie," Chris said. "But this is between you two. I'm open to however this develops."

Chris stepped out of the shower and walked away as Annie caught Tommy's stare. "What are you thinking, baby?" she asked.

"I'm thinking," he said, as his frown broke into a sexy smile. "That I love you both. And that won't change, whether the two of you form a relationship or not."

"So," she said.

"So," he echoed.

"We're going to try this thing?"

"I think we are," he said. "Should we start with a first date?"

"Like, a throuple first date?"

"I think so," he said. He chuckled. "I'm new at this, too, you know."

"That's true," she said with a smile. "Okay, how about you two pick me up at seven tomorrow night and take me out for a nice dinner. And we'll go from there."

"I love it," he said. "And I love you."

"I love you, too, Tommy." She kissed him deeply. "I can't wait for our second first date."

8

Second/First Date

When Annie heard the two knocks on her door, her stomach flipped about ten times. *Oh my God, they're here.*

She didn't know how this was going to go down, but she was excited to find out. She'd never been the kind of girl to back down from something different. She was always the first to try new foods, try new drinks, jump out of an airplane, or travel across the world alone. That's how she and Tommy had met in the first place. She had bought a ticket to Italy on a whim, just for the hell of it.

So why would this be any different? Why wouldn't she try this for Tommy? She loved him more than anyone in her life, including herself. If this might make him happy, she would try it. After all, she was the one who turned down his proposal.

But not because I didn't love him.

That was the rub. Even when she said no marriage, she hadn't been saying no to Tommy. She just hadn't been ready for it, damn it, when he got down on one knee. But it didn't mean she didn't want it *someday*. Maybe that day was now.

And maybe they needed to break up so they could have Chris. It wasn't what she would have wished for but, hot damn… *I like him.*

She could feel that deeply. This really wasn't just for Tommy, and she suspected that might be for the best. If she *only* did this for Tommy, that might lead to resentment. Even feeling used. So, the fact that she was attracted to Chris, that she wanted to explore something with Chris, too, felt better. Because now, it really was something that she wanted, too, and it wasn't only for Tommy.

"Hi," she said breathily as she swung open the door. The breeze lightly moved her long, blonde locks. One side was pulled up with a diamond clip, the other dangled lightly over her large, supple breasts. Her soft mounds were caged into an emerald-green corset dress that barely covered her ass.

"Good God," Chris said as his breath caught.

She smiled at him, feeling her pussy start to melt at his heated gaze as it landed on her eyes, lips, breasts.

"Annie," Tommy barely got her name out as he took in her small, tight figure, her breasts moving in time with her deep breaths.

She was already wanting them both. Tommy, in his navy blue vintage Christian Dior suit, the one she loved him in. His dark hair was loose, falling over his dark eyes, and his olive skin was glowing with excitement.

Then there was Christopher, in a sleek, black Armani suit and tie, his golden locks perfectly coiffed in their familiar wave, off his beautiful face, showing off his sparkling blue eyes.

She could see that both of them were already firm between their legs. The dynamic was set. The two men wanted each other, sure, but they both also wanted her. It was hard to stave off the desire to invite them both in and have them both fill her up, one in each wet, pink hole, driving her to an intense orgasm.

"We should go," Christopher choked out. "Before we don't leave at all."

This time when he looked at her, she could see a dangerous attraction, one that could consume her sexually. She knew now what Tommy saw in him. She saw that, too. A dark, sensual side that could make a girl's pussy orgasm for days.

"Yeah, let's go," said Tommy. He winged out his elbow. Annie shut the door and locked it before popping her clutch under her arm and sliding her hand into the crook of his elbow. As she did, she felt Chris's large hand wrap around her free one. His grip was intoxicating as she met his hungry stare with her own.

When they got to the car, the driver opened the door for them and the three climbed in as they headed to dinner.

~~~

They were at a table in the best restaurant in town, where the average Joe had to wait months to get in. But not with Tommy. Tommy's trust fund assured them the best tables and accommodations anywhere they went.

"Miss?" The hostess pointed to a small round table with a wrap-around booth. It was in its own private area of the restaurant, away from prying eyes, and bathed in candlelight, dark and romantic. She slid in to the middle and each man took a place beside her.

"You look beautiful," Tommy whispered as Chris ordered wine for the table. His gaze dropped to her breasts. "And sexy."
~~~

"I want them in your mouth later," she whispered back. She couldn't help it. She was going to have them both pleasure her tonight. No sex, of course. Not yet. It was the same rule she had for any first date. But her dripping wet folds made it clear to her that feeling their mouths and fingers over, and inside, her body was something she wanted.

"Fuck, baby," he whispered. "You're making me hard."

Tommy took her hand and placed it on his cock so she could feel him.

"Mmm," she murmured as Chris turned his attention to them.

"Hey now," he said with a sexy smile. "Don't start without me."

He leaned into Annie, smiling as he gazed at her face and lips. "You're stunning," he whispered. He lightly brushed his lips against hers.

She let out a little gasp of pleasure and surprise. "So are you."

"Mmm." He dragged his index finger up and down her thigh as she gently massaged Tommy's cock through his pants.

"Your wine," the waitress interrupted as they all pulled back a little. She filled the glasses halfway. "Would you like to know this evening's specials?"

"I already know what I want," Annie said boldly and seductively without looking at either man. "I want lobster." She touched Tommy's thigh under the table. "And steak." She touched Christopher's thigh.

"Excellent choice," the waitress said. "And for you two gentlemen?"

"We'll have the same," Tommy said in a heady voice.

"Great," she said. "I'll be out shortly with your salads."

As the waitress walked away, Annie's stroke on each man's thigh became a little deeper and closer to their cocks. Sensing her urgency, Tommy was the first to take her mouth in his and kiss her deeply as Christopher leaned in and slid his tongue in her ear, then down her neck.

"Fuck, you're beautiful," Chris breathed. "I'm not gonna be able to make it through dinner without making you come."

"Yes," she panted quietly as Tommy's mouth moved from her lips to her neck. Christopher was the first to slide his fingers between her thighs. Hoping for just this experience, she hadn't bothered to wear panties. She wanted him inside her. She'd start with his fingers, but, someday, she was going to need his cock. "Chris, yes."

She tried to maintain some degree of composure above the table, but below it, she'd already spread her legs while Chris explored her wetness.

"Fuck, you're wet," he breathed.

"Yes," she moaned lightly.

"Do you want me to make you come, Annie?" he growled in her ear.

"Yes," she moaned into his ear, biting it lightly and sucking it as he pushed two more fingers into her pussy. "Fuck me with your fingers, Chris."

To the outside world, it looked like a passionate kiss. But to the three of them, it was about making Annie come.

Not to be outdone, Tommy put his hand behind her back and slid it down below, parting her ass. Not like it was hard. The dress barely reached the bottom of her cheeks, so when she sat, it pulled up, exposing her cheeks. And with her legs spread, her pink, tight hole was open for business.

"Yes, Tommy," she whispered, trying to hold her expression steady as his finger found her tightness and started to massage it with a deep, penetrating finger. "Fuck, baby, yes."

"Come on our fingers, baby," Tommy whispered. His face never looking like he was fingering her ass under this table.

"Annie, come all over our fingers," Chris prompted. His lips brushing hers lightly like he wasn't pounding her pussy with three fingers.

"Yes," she choked quietly. "Fuck, yes. Fuck, yes. I'm coming."

Annie had never come so hard as she did on their fingers. Her tight pink hole and her pussy both throbbing with pleasure as the orgasm raced through her body at a steady, strong clip.

"Holy shit," she whispered. She should win an award for the act she was putting on above the table, because underneath it she was a throbbing, soaking mess.

"That was amazing," Chris whispered as he kissed Annie.

She loved it. She loved Chris kissing her, she loved him pounding her with his thick fingers, she loved him looking at her like that.

Tommy. God she was in love with him. She loved the way he cared for, that he knew her body and what she wanted, and that he would give anything to make her happy.

These two men were quickly becoming something special to her. As her relationship with Tommy was growing and changing into something deeper, her relationship

with Chris was new and exciting.
To have them both at the same time
was a wild, uncontrollable,
beautiful feeling.

"I think we should hit the
bathrooms," Tommy said with a
smile.

"Agreed," Chris said with a
laugh. "Dinner should be here
when we get back, and then, dessert
at your place?"

His steamy gaze at Annie told
her everything she needed to know.
And as she looked at Tommy with
love in her eyes, she knew he felt
the same way. Both men wanted
what she wanted.

"Absolutely," she said. "I've got
enough dessert for both of you."

9

Dessert for Three

It took only a moment once they were inside the condo for Chris's hands to unzip her dress and reach around to start massaging her naked breasts. She couldn't contain the gasp of pleasure that escaped her throat.

"Chris," she said passionately. "Yes, Chris, yes."

His thumbs erotically rubbed her nipples bringing them to attention and achingly sending waves of pleasure through her body.

"Annie, I want you so bad," he choked out. He pressed his hard, thick cock into her back and kissed her neck with a slow, burning movement up and down from her ear to her collarbone.

It was just a second before Tommy joined in, sliding his hands up her thighs and pushing her dress up so he could start tasting her wet pussy.

"Not yet," she said, pulling away from both of them as they stared at her. Feeling each of their hot gazes on her breasts and pussy, she used each of her hands to cover both. "Tonight is about exploring. Without sex. I'm not ready…just yet…for that."

"Okay, baby," Tommy said as Chris nodded his head.

"Of course, Annie, I'm sorry," Chris said. And she could see in both of them that they were sorry they had pushed a little harder than she was ready for.

"Dinner was so lovely," she said quietly as she put her dress back into place. "Learning about your family, Chris. Catching up on how your family is, Tommy."

She smiled at them with a shrug. "I don't want this to be a fleeting thing," she said with a confident voice. "If we're going to do this, I really want to do it. I want to know you, Chris. And I want to know you again, Tommy, like this."

"It was wonderful getting to know you, too, Annie," Chris said. His smile was so genuine. And then a touch of humor lit his eyes. "I mean, now that I know you and Tommy are both afraid of spiders, I guess I'm the designated spider killer in this relationship."

His lightness cut the tension so they could each catch their breath.

"Yeah, and since neither of you can cook for shit, I guess I'll be the one cooking and planning meals," Tommy said with a light laugh.

"You really can cook, baby," Annie said with a grin.

"Yes, you can," Christopher agreed. He wrapped his arms

around Tommy from behind and kissed his neck lightly, then his lips. Annie could feel her insides start to swirl at the sweet gesture.

"And what do I get to do?" she asked with a sultry tone. She slowly unzipped her dress again and let it slide off her body.

"Fuck, Annie," Chris said through an exhale.

"You're so fucking beautiful, baby," Tommy said. He started toward her. "You can just enjoy the ride."

"I like that idea," she said as Tommy dropped to his knees in front of her. He spread her pussy folds with his tongue as he flicked her clit. It sent waves of pleasure through her tight body.

"Tommy, yes," she moaned. She reached up her hands and started rubbing her nipples.

"Let me help you with that," Chris said gruffly. He moved

quickly toward her and took a nipple in his mouth while his hand stroked the other nipple.

She gasped with pleasure as she took the opportunity to grab onto Tommy's dark hair and guide his mouth on her sweet spot.

"Tommy, yes," she said. She gripped his hair harder. "Let me ride your mouth, baby."

"Mmmm, fuck yes." Tommy stood up. As Chris let go of Annie, Tommy wrapped his hands around her taut waist and lifted her onto his body, carrying her to the kitchen table. He sat her down gently then climbed on with her, lying down next to her. "Fuck my mouth with your pussy, baby."

"Fuck, yes." She turned and crawled onto his face, spreading her legs over his mouth until his tongue was sliding in her slit. His lips worked her clit and sensitive places moving from sucking to

licking in an agonizingly slow and
steady pace. "Tommy!"

She slid her hips back and forth
across his tongue, letting him
explore every inch of her. As she
could feel her orgasm start to flame
inside her, she glanced at Chris
with a heat that could melt butter.

"Chris," she said as she gripped
her nipples.

"Baby," he said as joined them.
He kissed her deeply and squeezed
her nipples with a rough touch that
made her moan in his mouth. "Tell
me what you want, Annie."

"I want your cock in my mouth,"
she said as she rode Tommy's
tongue, the orgasm building into a
raging fire about to explode.

"Fuck," he panted. He stripped
off his suit in a flash like a
superhero in a rush to save the
world. He jumped on top of the
table and slowly started to put his
cock in her mouth. "Oh, Annie."

She slowly took it in, gripping the base of his cock with both hands as she slowly moved them up and down his shaft. Her mouth took him deeper and deeper.

"Annie," he panted, as she took him deep in her throat. Her orgasm was on the edge now as she swallowed him down. He was huge and she couldn't take all of him, but she didn't need to. She could see by the look on his face he was ready to come. "I'm gonna come, baby."

He tried to pull out, but she held him right there in her mouth, licking and sucking and swallowing that thick meat until she felt the familiar pulse in his cock and his salty come dripping down her throat.

"Annie!" he screamed with pleasure. He gripped her hair and rocked his hips as he came and came and came. "Holy fucking shit."

As soon as he finished, she stopped riding Tommy as he moaned in protest.

"Don't worry, baby," she said with heat. "Let's come together."

She stood and twisted around, sitting back on his face with her ass toward him as she leaned down and took his cock in her mouth.

"Annie, fuck!" Tommy screamed with pleasure as she gave him the same treatment, gripping his cock with a strong stroke as she took the tip and the upper part of his cock deep in her throat. "Baby, I'm gonna come."

Tommy knew her deal. Knew that she loved to swallow, so he let it ride as he ate her tight, pink hole, eliciting a deep moan from her as her orgasm tipped over the edge. She groaned as an unbelievable wave of pleasure ravaged her body at the same time he came down her throat. He always tasted so good, so salty.

When he was done, she pulled away and twisted back to them on her knees, both men smiling with pleasure.

"Well," she asked. "How do you feel about sleeping together?"

~~~

When Annie woke up the next morning in her tiny black teddy, still a throuple virgin as she had intended, she was cuddled from behind by Tommy and wrapped in a figure eight to the front with Christopher. He was already awake and eyeing her with a smile.

"Morning, beautiful," he whispered.
~~~

She quickly took the sheet between them and folded it over his mouth, before putting a portion of it over her own mouth.

"Morning breath," she mumbled through the sheet as Chris's eyes lit with humor.

He gripped her ass and chuckled. "Right."

"I hate those movies and books that act like the romantic leads never wake up with bad breath," she whispered with a laugh. "Like, come on, brush those teeth!"

A low laugh rose up from his chest as their eyes met.

"You're funny," he said. She couldn't see it, but she knew he was smiling behind the sheet. His eyes had a way of crinkling at the corners when he was grinning. She already loved that about him.

Whoa. I'm starting to get the feels for Chris. She peered into his eyes and could see he was maybe thinking the same thing.

"Wanna try and cook breakfast?" he whispered.

"Or," she whispered back. "We can order it."

"I like your idea better."

They quietly laughed together again before he pulled on her hip and nodded to slide out of bed. She followed him across the silk sheets, grabbing her phone, as they tip-toed into the bathroom and clicked the door shut.

She reached into the closet and grabbed a new toothbrush and handed it to him as he laughed.

"You're serious about this, aren't you?"

She nodded as she put her phone on the counter and picked up her toothbrush, putting toothpaste on it.

"Does this mean no kissing after partaking in your private parts?" He opened the toothbrush packet and plopped a good size portion of toothpaste onto the brush.

"Correct," she answered.

"Oh my God," he said stopping just before the brush hit his mouth. "You're the reason why Tommy always brushes his teeth after he goes down on me."

"You're welcome," she sang before sliding the toothbrush in her mouth and brushing every surface, including her tongue and gums.

"Huh," he said, sliding the toothbrush into his mouth and scrubbing.

"What?" she asked as she spit and started brushing again.

He spit a bit of toothpaste out. "I don't mind the taste," he said with a shrug. "I like it, actually. I think it's sexy."

"Pussy might be sexy, but ass is not," she said rinsing her toothbrush and putting it away. "It's ass, Chris. No, thank you."

He laughed in surprise and spit out everything in his mouth, cracking up even more when he looked at her. "Jesus, Annie."

He rinsed his mouth and brush then dropped the brush on the counter with a soft click. He walked over to her with a broad smile and took her in his arms.

Holy shit, this feels so good. And natural. She leaned into him, staring into his blue eyes with the gaze of a woman who was starting to fall in love.

"I think I could be getting the feels for you, Annie," he said softly as he leaned down and gently kissed her lips.

"I think I could be catching feels for you, too, Christopher," she said, kissing him gently.

"I love it when you call me by my full name," he whispered.

"Christopher," she whispered in his ear.

"Fuck," he moaned softly.

She could feel his cock starting to get firm as he pulled away.

"Chris?"

He turned his back to her and she could hear him exhale before he turned back around to face her.

"Annie, I want you," he said as his eyes roamed her body. "But, like you, I want to do this right. I love Tommy. More than anything. And I can feel I'm starting to fall for you. So."

"So?" she asked.

"So," he said, grabbing her phone and giving it a shake, "Let's order breakfast and wake up our man."

When Christopher said "our man" a shiver ran through her. She loved hearing him say that. Tommy *was* theirs. And with time, she hoped, maybe they could all be each other's.

10

The Ring

The next two months felt like a dream. Annie fell hard and fast for Christopher, and he fell hard for her, too. They hadn't said, "I love you," but it was close. She knew all about his family, his life, and she'd even had lunch with his sister. It was official: they were crazy for each other, and both of them were crazy for Tommy.

Tommy was, of course, different now. The basics of who he was a year ago were still the same, but with little changes. Probably from growing through a break-up, probably from being around Chris and picking up some of his idiosyncrasies, and probably because he was older and wiser.

Annie took her time trying to get to know Tommy as the new man he was now. He liked green beans instead of peas. He preferred working out in the morning instead of at night. He had a new way he liked his cock stroked to bring him over the edge.

She learned all of it. She wanted nothing more than to please him and make him happy and, if she was being honest with herself, make him take that damn Tiffany's box off the fireplace and put the ring on her finger.

She glanced at the hearth and the blue box on top of it.

What the fuck is it gonna take?

She didn't realize exactly how ready she was to marry Tommy until the night he brought that Chinese food over a little more than two months ago. She knew then, he was it for her. Even now, even with Christopher in their lives, it was still Tommy she wanted to call her husband.

"Annie?"

She broke her gaze from the fireplace and turned to look into Tommy's eyes.

"Tommy," she said with surprise. "I didn't even hear you come in."

"Sorry," he said.

She was trying to decipher the look on his face but couldn't quite put her finger on it. *Is he mad? Upset? What is that?*

"What's wrong, baby?" She stepped toward him and he immediately took a step back. "Tommy?"

She stopped and stared at him, confused. They had come so far, the three of them. *What could this possibly be about?*

"I think we need to talk, Annie," he said.

"Okay," she said. "About what?"

He glanced over at the fireplace. "About what you were staring at."

He walked over to the fireplace and picked up the Tiffany box, blowing the dust off it and turning to face her with it.

The memories came rushing back to her. Him on his knee asking her to marry him, her saying no, him moving out, and the twelve terrible months that followed until he showed up with Chinese food and Christopher.

Tears stung her eyes seeing him holding it now. "Tommy?"

"I'm not going to ask you to marry me, Annie," he said.

"You're being cruel."

"I'm being honest," he said. He moved toward her and put the ring in his jacket pocket. "Annie, things are so different now. In a good way. I know you can feel that. But I catch you, staring at that damn ring. And I can't help but think...I keep thinking that you believe it's going to go back to that. It's not. And we need to talk about that."

She didn't want to cry, but, damn it, she couldn't stop herself. The tears burst from her eyes as her sobs erupted. "Tommy." She cried as he wrapped his arms around her.

"I'm sorry, Annie," he said. "I love you so damn much. But the old us, the two people in love who were headed toward marriage, that's gone now. In its place are two men who want to be with you, who want you to be the center of our family, who want to love you. This new future…it's me *and* it's Christopher."

"But I want *you*, Tommy," she sobbed into his shirt, dampening it with her tears. She hadn't realized until this very moment that her motivation all along was Tommy and getting the future she had turned down.

He sighed as he kissed her hair and gently stroked it. "I know. That ring. It's never left that spot. You're still hanging onto the past. And I want you to move forward with me into a new future. With Christopher. Into something different. Can you let go of what we had?"

She wasn't sure she could. He was right, of course. As much as she cared about Christopher, as much as she wanted to tell him she loved him, the truth was that she was still madly, deeply in love with Tommy. She still viewed this whole situation as if Tommy was her man and Chris was along for the ride.

And now here was Tommy, telling her that was wrong. That the past she desperately wanted back was no longer available to her. It broke her heart. And it came out in a sudden burst as she pushed him away.

"Tommy," she sobbed. She ran down the hallway and slammed the bedroom door, locked it, and dropped onto her bed, weeping into her pillow as she started to let the past go.

~~~

When Annie woke up, it was midnight. She had cried herself to sleep under the weight of Tommy's request to let go of her dream of walking down the aisle in a clean, white dress and hearing him call her his wife in front of God and everyone.

She could feel the tears bubbling up again and she slowly climbed out of bed to grab a tissue and wipe
~~~

them away. As she did, her stomach growled. *Might as well eat something.* She pulled open the door and jumped back in surprise when Tommy came crashing backwards into her room.

"Tommy!" she yelled. Then Christopher jumped at her yell across the hall, banging his head on the wall and knocking a picture off its hook. "Christopher!"

"Fuck, Annie," Tommy groaned as he sat up, rubbing the back of his head.

"Holy shit, scream much?" Christopher said as he shook himself awake and rubbed the back of his head.

"What the fuck are you two doing?" she yelled as she walked into the hallway and picked up the picture. She centered it on its hook as she waited for them to answer. "Well?"

"Annie—"

"What? Come to tell me I can't expect children, either? That you two are gonna get married? That *I'm* the one who's a third wheel?" Get the fuck out."

She stormed down the hallway and into the kitchen, pulling out an egg pan, spraying it with butter and dropping it onto the burner, turning it all the way to ten. She grabbed the eggs from the fridge as the two men stumbled in.

"Want me to cook that for you, baby?" Tommy asked.

"Don't call me that," she said. "You don't mean it."

"Annie, I do mean it," he said gently. "More than you can possibly understand."

"You wanted a future with *me*, Tommy," she said as she slammed her own chest. "Me. Children. Marriage. The whole thing. I just wasn't ready then. I'm ready now."

She was begging and she hated that. It felt out of character for her. *Where the fuck is this coming from?*

"Yes, but now *I'm* not ready," Tommy said, the pain streaking across his face. "I love you both. I want you both. I want to make it work, but it just won't be the traditional way, Annie. The way you pictured. Or even I pictured. Can't you understand?"

"Yes, I do understand," she yelled as the egg pan started to smoke. "You don't want me!"

"The pan!" Christopher yelled as he moved toward the stove.

Annie beat him to it, knocking it off the stove. As it started to fall, she grabbed for it, catching the hot side in her right hand and screaming in pain. "Fuck!"

"Annie!" Tommy yelled. He grabbed her by the waist and dragged her to the kitchen faucet as he turned on a cold stream of water and ran her hand under it.

She began to sob again as Christopher shut off the stove and picked up the pan, letting it cool on the back burner.

"I'll be right back," he said. Annie and Tommy heard the front door open and shut as the silence overtook them. Her light sniffles were the only thing cutting through the air.

"Annie, I'm sorry. For all of it. I promised you I'd take care of your heart," he said. "I intend to keep that promise."

He shut off the water and gently dried her hand with a kitchen towel. He took the ring box from his jacket pocket, opened it with a creak, and pulled out her platinum engagement ring with a five-carat round diamond. Her eyes overflowed again with tears as he slid it on her left ring finger.

"I made you a promise, Annie, when I asked for your hand in marriage," he said. "And I swore I'd never hurt you. That I'd protect your heart."

She stared at the ring. It was beautiful. And it was exactly what she wanted. She wanted to wear Tommy's ring and be his and only his. And she didn't even realize that was what she truly wanted until the ring was on her finger.

Wait. Is it?

Suddenly she felt it. She knew this wasn't right. Not only was he putting this ring on her finger out of a sense of duty and obligation to her, but he was betraying the way he felt about Christopher. And if she was honest with herself, it was betraying the way *she* felt about Christopher, too.

Fuck. I've really, truly fallen for Christopher.

"Tommy—"

"Oh," Christopher interrupted as he stared at the ring on her finger.

"No, Christopher, it's not…" she uttered.

"I should go," he said.

Tommy said nothing, the pain in his eyes so deep that she wanted to die right then and there.

Christopher put down a first aid kit on the counter and walked away.

"Let him go," Tommy said. "He needs time. I think we all do."

11

Three Is Just Right

It had been a solid seven days and Annie still hadn't heard from Christopher or Tommy.

She'd spent that time oscillating between wearing her ring and reading bridal magazines as unfettered joy ran through her with sobbing uncontrollably into her pillow for hours on end, staring at her ring on the nightstand as she thought about losing Tommy or Christopher, or both.

Shit was falling apart in her home and her work life. Her latest job as a party planner had been missing the cake and she was lucky she had fucked the baker at a shop down the street so she could get a last-minute delivery and save her own ass.

"Fuck," she moaned out loud to no one. It was time to fix this and she knew she was the only who could. It was *her* inability to let go of the past that was causing this fucking problem. No matter how untraditionally she'd lived her life up to this moment, she was, apparently, still glued to this traditional idea of marriage and relationships. And no matter how much she loved Tommy and now Christopher, she was having a hard time separating herself into a new kind of normal. One that worked for all of them.

She sat up in bed with a new sense of determination. "Get your ass up, bitch, and do something about it."

And she knew exactly what had to be done.

~~~

At precisely 7 p.m., Annie's doorbell rang. She spritzed on a touch of perfume as she caught a glimpse of her long golden locks falling down onto her ample breasts. Tonight, they were wrapped in a simple pink tank top that landed just above her snug, indigo jeans. She eagerly swung open the door and smiled.

"Hi Christopher," she said.

He caught his breath as he ran his eyes over her firm body. "Jesus, Annie," he gasped with pleasure. His stare immediately went to her soft breasts, then up to her necklace. "That looks pretty on you."
~~~

She reached up and touched it with a smile. "Thank you. Come in."

"Annie—"

"Christopher," she said firmly. "Please come in."

He nodded as he walked inside following her to the bar cart in the living room. She poured him his favorite whiskey, neat, and one for herself. She handed him the smooth liquor and they clinked glasses as they each took a sip. The brown liquid warmed her from her mouth to her pussy as she let his gaze wander from her face to her breasts, to between her legs and back again.

She put down her glass, then took his and put it down, stepping into him and letting her body talk for her as she rubbed against him.

"Annie," he said headily. "Fuck."

It only took a minute for him to unleash her breast and wrap his mouth around her nipple, sucking and nibbling it until she panted with pleasure.

"Christopher, wait," she said, grabbing his hair and pulling it up as her tank top slid back into place.

"I'm sorry," he said.

"No, don't be sorry," she said. "I want you, too."

"You do?"

"Of course," she said as she looked deep into his eyes. "Christopher. I love you."

"Annie," he said as a smile spread across his face. He slid both of his hands into her hair and pulled her close. "I love you, too."

He gently brushed his lips against hers before sinking his tongue deep inside her mouth and kissing her like a man on fire. He pulled back as they both caught their breath.

"I've been wanting to tell you," he said quietly.

"I know, me too," she said.

"But then," he touched her right hand, which was loosely wrapped with a bandage, then glanced at her left hand. "Wait, where's your ring?"

"Annie?"

They both turned to see Tommy standing there, staring at them.

"Tommy," she said with a breath of relief. She moved slowly toward him. As she did, she saw his eyes drop to the necklace and a slow smile started to spread across his face.

"Annie," he said as he moved toward her and enveloped her into a hug.

She knew that Tommy knew as soon as he saw her necklace that it was the diamond he bought her. That she had taken something beautiful from their past and made it into something beautiful for their future.

"I'm sorry, Tommy," she said.

"No, Annie, I'm sorry," he said. "That I put you in this situation."

"I went willingly," she said. "And I fell in love with you all over again. And I fell in love with Christopher. And it took me a minute to grieve our past, and give up stupid things like wearing a beautiful white gown and—"

"Those things aren't stupid, Annie," he interrupted. "And it's okay to want them. Even have them. Why can't you wear a wedding gown and walk down the aisle for a commitment ceremony?"

"I," she had to stop and think about that. *Why the fuck hadn't she thought of that?* She shrugged. "I guess, I don't know, I guess I could."

"You think I don't wanna see you come down the aisle toward

me? Wearing that dress. Telling everyone we love that the three of us are committing to each other?"

"Oh," she said with surprise. "I didn't think of it that way."

She turned and looked at Christopher, who had tears in his eyes. She reached out her hand as he took it and stepped toward them. He kissed Annie first, then Tommy. They hugged tightly before Christopher gently pulled back.

"I'm sorry, baby," he said to Tommy. "I shouldn't have run away. I should have talked to you."

"Me, too," Tommy said. "I'm sorry, Chris."

"I know." They gently kissed before looking back to Annie.

"What about kids?" she asked. "Not to dampen the mood but I need to know."

"I want a baby," said Tommy. "I've always wanted a baby with you, Annie."

It made her stomach tingle when he said it. "Me, too, baby."

She gazed at Christopher. "What about you, Chris?"

"I'd like to have a baby," he said quietly. "But I'm open to a bigger discussion about how we want to do it. How it all might unfold."

"Okay," she nodded. "I can work with that."

The tension of what had transpired between them dissipated from the air as it was replaced by a deep longing to make their relationship official. Christopher was the first to act, stepping toward Annie and pulling her into his arms.

"Annie," he said. He kissed her deeply and slowly worked his hands over her breasts, pinching and squeezing the nipples until she moaned with pleasure. "I want you, baby."

"I want you, too, Christopher," she said seductively as she turned to gaze at Tommy. "And you, too, baby."

~~~

It felt perfectly natural for the three of them to be naked together on the brand-new King-sized bed and mattress in their bedroom.

"Baby, is this new?" Tommy asked.

"New beginnings, right?" she said as she slid up the satin sheets to him, straddled his hips and rubbed her nipples. "For the three of us."

"Fuck yes," he said. He sat up and dipped his head down, taking her breasts in his hands, and sucking on one nipple, then the
~~~

other, as she moaned. "God, I love your tits, baby."

"Me, too," Christopher said as he slid in behind her and reached his hands around her taut stomach before sliding them down to her soaking wet pussy. "But not as much as this tight little pussy."

"Yes," she panted as Tommy's mouth traded between her aching nipples and Christopher's finger sunk deep into her wetness, first one finger, then two.

"Tell us what you want, baby," Christopher breathed into her ear as he pulsed his finger in and out, slow and steady.

"I want you in my pussy," she groaned to Christopher. "And I want you in my tight, pink ass," she panted as she held Tommy's gaze.

"Whatever you want, baby," Tommy said as he lifted her up and laid her down on the bed, on her side.

She gasped as both men started to kiss and lick her from her head to her toes. Christopher took the front as Tommy took the back. "Yes!" she moaned as Tommy buried his tongue in her tight, pink hole. "Tommy!"

She reached around and grabbed his hair as he worked her ass until it started to blossom for him. Just then, she felt Christopher lift her leg over his head and bury his tongue in her pussy. "Christopher, yes!"

She let go of Tommy's hair and grabbed Christopher's, moving her hips as she dipped her pussy into Chris's tongue, then her ass into Tommy's tongue.

"Fuck me," she panted. "Please, fuck me!"

Christopher moved first, sliding beside her and waiting for Tommy to move before he laid her on her back. "Annie," he panted. "I want you so bad, baby."

It was her first time with Christopher, and she wanted it so badly. She loved him and she wanted to show him just how much.

"Baby," she said as she framed his face with her hands. "I love you so much."

He slowed down and smiled at her. "I love you, too, Annie. So much, baby."

She spread her legs and thrust her hips up to touch his hard cock. "I want you, baby."

"Fuck," he moaned. "Fuck, I want you, too."

He slowly pushed the tip of his huge, thick cock into her wet pussy. "Fuck!"

"Christopher!" she moaned. "Fuck, you feel so good."

"Baby, yes," he groaned. He slowly pushed himself in and then out, in and then out, rocking with her hips to push him deeper into wetness. "Annie, you're so tight."

"Christopher, you feel so good," she panted as she squeezed his cock with her tight little pussy. "More!"

"Yes!" he groaned as one final thrust pushed him all the way in. "Holy shit, I'm all the way in you, baby."

Annie could barely contain herself. She loved Chris, she loved him inside of her, and she wanted this. But not without Tommy. She glanced over to where he had been and found him working his cock with his hand, a grin on his face as he watched the two of them.

"Tommy," she moaned. "Tommy, fuck me."

"Whatever you want, baby," he said. Just like he always had. He would give her anything she wanted, and he had. And then some.

When Tommy came over, he stopped at Christopher and gave him a deep kiss as Chris thrust himself deep inside her.

"Yes," she panted as she watched them. They were so sexy together, and they were hers. Tommy pulled away and turned to Annie with a smile.

"You ready for both of us, baby?"

His words were filled with double meanings. Was she ready for them sexually? *God yes.* Was she ready for the three of them to be a throuple? *Oh, hell yes.* Was she ready for them to be her everything in a new future of their making?

"Fuck yes, baby," she said.

With that, Christopher reached his hands under her hips and rolled her onto his cock as he rolled onto his back.

"Yes," she moaned, rocking her hips and riding his cock as he penetrated deep inside her.

"Annie," Christopher panted as she felt him stiffen even harder inside of her.

Just then, Annie felt Tommy behind her, fingering her tight hole and opening her up.

"Baby, yes!" She started to rock between Tommy's fingers and Chris's cock, as a pleasure beyond her wildest dreams began to erupt inside of her. "Fuck me, Tommy!"

And he did. He pulled out his fingers then slowly pulsed and pushed his throbbing cock into her ass, moving with Chris's rhythm until finally, she was filled with both of them.

"Holy shit," she screamed. "This feels so amazing."

"Yes, Annie, yes, ride my cock," Chris moaned.

"Annie, you're so tight,"
Tommy panted.

She took control and started to slide her pelvis between them both, rocking onto Chris's cock and then pulsing back onto Tommy's cock. Once they felt her rhythm, they moved with her, and within seconds they were all on the verge of coming.

"Annie, I wanna come in you, baby," Chris moaned.

"I wanna come in you, too, baby," Tommy whispered in her ear as she took his cock deep in her ass.

"Yes," she panted. "Come in me, both of you. Own me!"

"Yes!" Tommy yelled as Annie rocked harder and harder against both of their cocks.

"I'm coming," Tommy screamed as she rocked hard into him and he gripped her hips.

"I'm coming, too," Chris yelled. She rocked onto his cock and he grabbed her hips.

She kept her motions to quick small movements that ramped up her orgasm. "I'm coming!" she yelled.

And she did, the strongest orgasm she'd ever had in her life as it rippled through her body, followed by another, and then another. They all collapsed exhausted into bed together. Annie grinned.

"That was amazing," she sighed.

Both men wrapped their arms around her with smiles on their faces.

"I love you, Annie," Tommy said.

"I love you, too, baby," Chris said.

"I love you both," Annie said as her breathing steadied.

"I love you, too, Chris," Tommy said with a big smile.

"Baby," Chris said, "I love you so fucking much."

They leaned over Annie and kissed each other deeply. When they released, they gave Annie sweet kisses before they all fell asleep together, just like that.

When they woke up the next morning, they were an official throuple in love.

And Annie couldn't have been happier if she tried.

12

What Happens Next?

No one at the fucking brunch table breathed, blinked or moved as the waitress brought another round of drinks.

"Holy. Fucking. Shit," Summer finally said, completely impressed. And Annie knew how hard it was to impress Summer. "I'm mother fuckin' speechless. You fucking win life, Annie."

She clinked her glass against Annie's, then slugged the rest of her drink back in one toss. "Fuck me."

"Annie," Fawn said quietly as she leaned in a little more. "I mean, what happens next?"

"Um, hello?" Tabitha spoke up, flicking her fingernails in the air like a drama queen. "Am I the only fucking one who's thinking why the fuck didn't you tell us this sooner you clever slut?"

Annie had to laugh at Tabitha's honesty. She was right, of course, they'd had several brunches since this all started and Annie hadn't said a word.

"Because." Annie shrugged. "I didn't know what I wanted. And I didn't want to hear anyone else's opinion until I knew what *my* opinion was. And what the relationship was. But, you know, last night, we made it real. We made it official. So…now you know."

"So, you're in a throuple? Like, a real one?" asked Summer.

"Yeah," Annie said. She took a sip of her drink. "I'm in a throuple relationship."

So weird saying that.

"Okay, how does it work?"
Fawn asked.

"No idea," Annie laughed. "I
suppose I'll find out."

"Would you have a fucking baby
with each of them?" Tabitha asked
as her heavily made-up face
furrowed into a frown, her head
tilting to the side.

"I'd consider it, yes," Annie
said. And she meant it. *Holy shit, I
really do mean that.* "I love them. I
love both of them."

"And you'd do a commitment
ceremony?" Fawn pushed.

"If it came to that, I think I
would," Annie said. She smiled as
a vision of her in a white gown and
her loves in their suits flashed in
her head. Her whole body warmed
at the thought. "I don't think we're
there quite yet. But, maybe,
someday."

"Well, I'm fucking impressed,"
Summer said as she leaned back

hard into the booth. "I also feel like I need to see Chris's cock."

"Fucking sign me up for that," Tabitha said as she took a swig of her drink.

"Back off ladies," Annie said with a mildy threatening wink. "He's mine now. They both are."

"Well, I can't wait to see how this unfolds," Fawn said.

"Me too," Annie said. "Me, too."

Annie's love story isn't over! Keep reading the *Girls Who Brunch Erotic Series* to see what happens to Annie, Tommy, and Christopher! Wanna learn more about the other ladies—Summer, Fawn, and Tabitha? Keep reading the *Girls Who Brunch Erotic Series* as they have brunch, enjoy sex, and talk about it all!

Scan me